Bravo and Glee

of Cape Cod

Lee Farm Book

By Sharon Lee Mendes

Illustrated by Marguerite L. Miller

SUMMERLAND PUBLISHING

ISBN 978-0-9824870-8-2

For more information, visit www.SummerlandPublishing.com.
Printed in the U. S. A.

Library of Congress # 2011929957

Bravo gets a huge trophy and a beautiful garland of roses.

He also gets lots of carrots with his hugs.

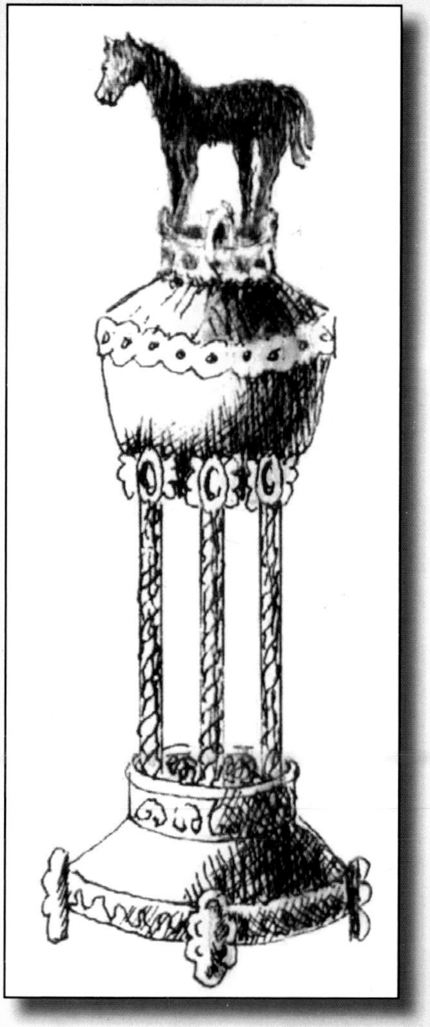

He is so happy because he knows
he did his very best.

Chapter 6
What Happened to Bravo?

One morning on a summer's day, my two best friends were kicking up their heels and running around the paddock. The grass was high and Bravo did not see the big rock. He smashed into it and fell down. Miss Sharon came running. She could see that he was badly hurt. She called the veterinarian, Dr. Jesse, to come and help. Dr. Jesse said that Bravo had broken his leg. She put a cast on it to hold his leg in place. He was helped to stand up and was walked very slowly into his stall. Dr. Jesse said it would be about six weeks of stall rest to heal Bravo's leg.

I knew I would have to do the most important job of my life.
I will have to stay close by Bravo's side day and night.

Glee helped me also because she kept Bravo happy.

We watched
the sun rise
in the morning.

We listened to the rain gently falling on the barn roof.

We watched the moon and the stars come out at night.

I chased all the “mousies” out of the barn.
Bravo stood so still and never looked scared.
I knew now that he was as brave as his name and had done his best.

Finally, Dr. Jesse said Bravo's cast could come off. Everyone was gathered around to see him. He walked slowly at first into the paddock. With Glee by his side, each day he became stronger. Then one day he was well enough to kick up his heels and run again.

Miss Sharon said Bravo would not be able to be a race horse anymore. So he did the next best thing.

Bravo became famous as a therapeutic riding horse.

Louie was one of his favorite students.

Chapter 7

Around the Barn, Again!

The rest of the summer went very well.

We had long sunny days with lots of trail rides and horse shows. I am back to long cat naps between "mousie" chasings. The 4H Club is helping with all activities and barn chores.

Now that Bravo is better, can you guess what I am doing?

I have time to raise a family.
I have four wonderful kittens. They are so fuzzy and soft and so full of energy. Someday they will be important barn cats, too.

~ THE END ~

About the Illustrator

Marguerite L. Miller is an award winning artist. She has many years of experience in watercolor painting, pen and ink drawing and acrylic. She has had one-woman shows and is represented in private collections. As a member of the Falmouth Artist Guild, she has served as a board member, a teacher and a volunteer for various activities. She resides on Cape Cod in the town of Mashpee.

About the Author

This is the first publication for local author Sharon Lee Mendes. She is a retired nurse who has always had a passion for writing. She is a certified riding instructor and has done apprentice work as a therapeutic riding instructor. Sharon has been given both bronze and silver 4H Clover Awards for her service with the Bourne Equestrians Riding Club. She resides on Cape Cod in the town of Pocasset.

Also Available From Summerland Publishing

Tid Bits

Gina La Monica, Ed.D.
978-0-9824870-4-4
US$16.95

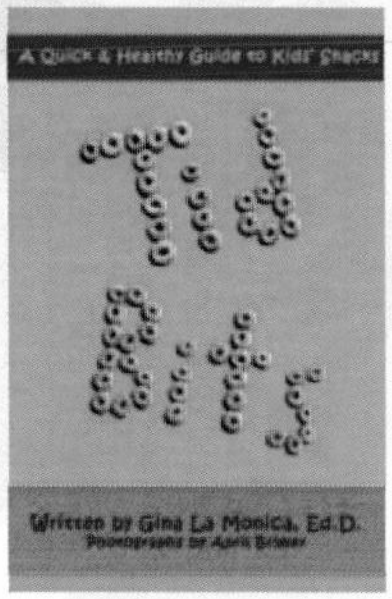

Tid Bits is an easy to read picture book of 26 healthy snacks for children. Parents can prepare these snacks in less than 5 minutes. There is even a grocery list at the back of the book to make shopping for these snacks that much easier. With the author being a health professor and exercise physiologist, she provides parents with educational information in the introduction along with educational websites. With the childhood obesity epidemic on the rise, this is a must read for all parents.

Lucky Me

Christi Dunlap
978-0-9795444-9-1
US$14.95

"Lucky Me", narrated by a rescued dog named Rocky, provides a guide to children and parents looking to add an animal companion to their family. Illustrated with full color photographs by the author, Rocky and his friends walk us through what a humane society can offer to animals, and what every animal guardian should know about caring for and keeping their new family member safe.

Kid Ethics

James "Bud" Bottoms
978-0-9794863-0-2
US$12.95

Much like learning the alphabet, children should be exposed to the formal education of ethics at a very early age to help them socialize in appropriate and respectful ways. Childhood is a time when these future citizens should acquire the skills and attitudes that result in respect and proper decorum.

"Kid Ethics" will help develop thoughtful, respectful, and caring citizens. One of the best features of this book is that it encourages the whole family to participate in these essential values.

Are You a Good Sport?

Wayne Soares
978-0-9795444-7-7
US$14.95

Are You A Good Sport? provides kids with key aspects of sportsmanship and character by using illustrations andrhymes. Wayne Soares just finished a season with his new TV show, The Sportsfan, a popular sports/comedy television program.

The Mountain Boy

Christina Pages
978-0-9794863-9-5
US$12.95

A wonderful story about a young boy and his love of nature. His unique ability to interact with all forms of nature is both endearing and educational for young readers.

Order from:
www.summerlandpublishing.com, www.barnesandnoble.com, www.amazon.com
or find them in your favorite bookstore!
Email SummerlandPubs@aol.com for more information.
Summerland Publishing, 21 Oxford Drive, Lompoc, CA 93436